The Foolis
Timid Rabbit

An Indian Folk Tale

written by Charlotte Guillain ☸ illustrated by Steve Dorado

Raintree is an imprint of Capstone Global Library Limited, a company incorporated in England and Wales having its registered office at 7 Pilgrim Street, London, EC4V 6LB – Registered company number: 6695582

www.raintree.co.uk
myorders@raintree.co.uk

Edited by Daniel Nunn, Rebecca Rissman, Sian Smith, and Gina Kammer
Designed by Joanna Hinton-Malivoire and Peggie Carley
Original illustrations © Capstone Global Library Ltd 2014
Illustrated by Steve Dorado
Production by Victoria Fitzgerald
Originated by Capstone Global Library Ltd
Printed and bound in India

ISBN 978 1 406 28134 7 (paperback)
18
10 9 8 7 6 5 4 3 2 1

ISBN 978 1 406 28141 5 (big book)
18 17 16 15 14
10 9 8 7 6 5 4 3 2 1

British Library Cataloguing in Publication Data
A full catalogue record for this book is available from the British Library.

Characters

Rujul the rabbit

Mukti the monkey

Deepa the deer

Ekram the
elephant

Lukesh the lion

One hot day, Rujul the rabbit was sleeping under a tree. As soon as he woke up, he began to worry. "What would happen if the world came to an end?" he wondered.

Mukti the monkey looked down from the tree and saw Rujul worrying. She laughed and threw a coconut down at him. Rujul jumped when he heard it fall behind him.

"The world is coming to an end!" he cried.

Rujul started to run without looking back.

Another rabbit saw him running and asked, "What are you running from?"

"The world is coming to an end!" shouted Rujul, and the other rabbit raced after him.

Soon they met another rabbit
that asked, "What are you
running from?"

"The world is coming to an end!"
yelled Rujul, and the other rabbit
ran after him too.

Every rabbit that saw them running began to panic. They followed Rujul as fast as they could.

Soon there were
hundreds of rabbits
racing around the forest.

When Deepa the deer saw all
the rabbits running, she asked,
"What are you running from,
little rabbits?"

"The world is coming to an end!"
shrieked Rujul.

Deepa gasped and
began to run after
him too.

Soon Ekram the elephant saw all the rabbits and Deepa running by, and he asked what was going on.

"The world is coming to an end!" cried Deepa.

Ekram gulped and thundered after the other animals.

Lukesh the lion was lying in the shade, when suddenly all the animals came stampeding past him. He roared, and they all stopped.

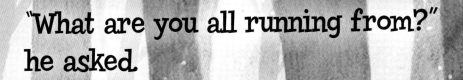

"What are you all running from?"
he asked.

"The world is coming to an end!"
the animals all replied.

"How do you know?"
asked Lukesh.

Ekram pointed at
Deepa and said,
"She told me!"

Deepa pointed at the rabbits
and said, "They told me!"

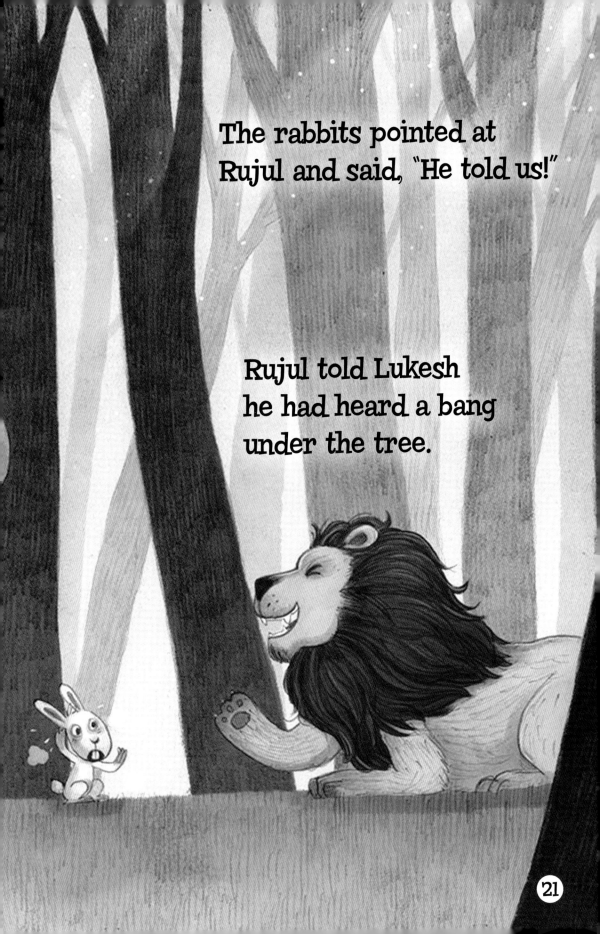

The rabbits pointed at
Rujul and said, "He told us!"

Rujul told Lukesh
he had heard a bang
under the tree.

Lukesh took Rujul back to the tree and pointed at the coconut. "That is what you heard! The world is not coming to an end, you foolish, timid rabbit!"

Lukesh roared with laughter, and Rujul leapt with fear and began to run again. And do you know what? He is still running, even to this day.

The end

The moral of the story

Many traditional stories have a moral. This is a lesson you can learn from the story. The moral of this story is that you should always remember to think for yourself before you believe a rumour or follow the crowd.

The origins of *The Foolish, Timid Rabbit*

Nobody knows who first told the story of *The Foolish, Timid Rabbit*, but the story comes from India. The story has been passed on by Indian storytellers over hundreds of years, with different storytellers making their own changes to it over time. People used to tell stories like this for entertainment before we had television, radio, or computers. Eventually, this tale was written down with other stories in a collection called the *Jataka*. People who follow the Buddhist religion believe the stories in the *Jataka* tell about the past lives of the Buddha, who founded the Buddhist religion.